I AM HERE

HERE

YO ESTOY AQUÍ

I AM HERE
HERE

YO ESTOY AQUÍ

BY ROSE BLUE

PICTURES BY MONETA BARNETT

FRANKLIN WATTS, INC.
845 THIRD AVENUE   NEW YORK, NEW YORK 10022

To my friend Renée —
with love and thanks

The wintry morning wind made Luz feel
very cold and she held tight to Maria's hand.
Luz took such long steps that her big sister
had to walk fast to keep up.

They hurried past The People's Fruit
Store, past the *bodega*, or grocery store,
and past a candy store where people were
sitting on stools eating breakfast as a
radio played Spanish music.

The music made Luz think of her
homeland, Puerto Rico, where it was
always warm and you never needed a
heavy coat. Luz's cheeks were wet.
Maybe the tears were because she felt
sad, or maybe it was the cold.

At last the girls reached school and went inside. Luz felt better for a minute, but when they got to the room marked Kindergarten, she felt bad again.

Maria gave her little sister a big hug good-bye, waved, and went off to find her own class.

Luz stood in the doorway and cried, louder and louder and louder.

A teacher came and took Luz's hand. Together, they walked into the room.

The teacher held out a puzzle and said, "Sit down, dear," but Luz kept standing.

The teacher's voice was soft but her words were strange. Luz was scared and she pulled away and walked to the other side of the room.

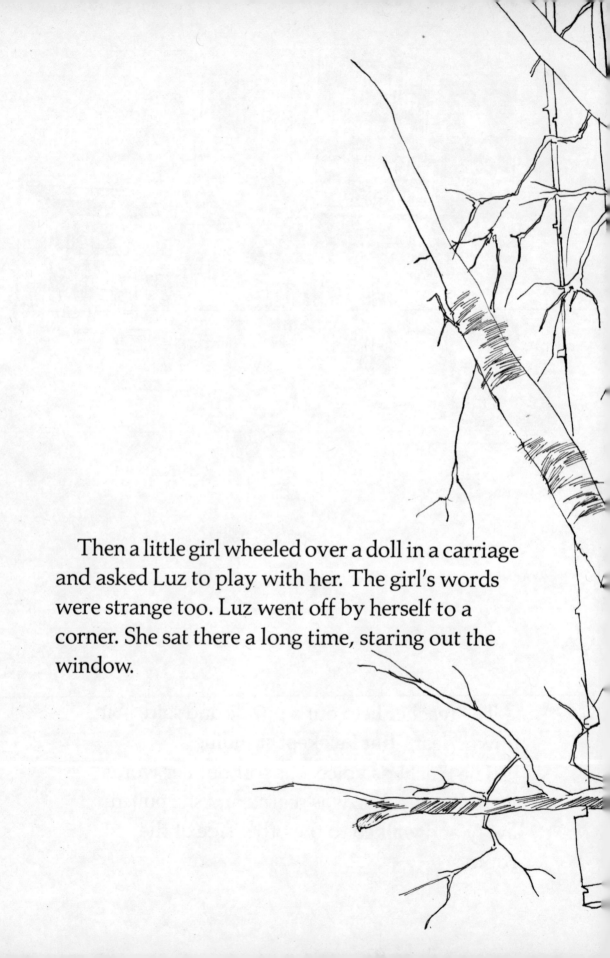

Then a little girl wheeled over a doll in a carriage and asked Luz to play with her. The girl's words were strange too. Luz went off by herself to a corner. She sat there a long time, staring out the window.

There were no leaves on the trees outside the
school. Luz thought of the green leaves on the
trees in Puerto Rico, and she started to cry all
over again.

Someone said, "Well, who is this?" Luz didn't
understand the words, but she looked up and
saw a woman standing nearby.

"That's the new girl," a boy answered. "She doesn't know how to talk."

"Oh, yes, she does," the woman said. And then she went on to say, *"Me llamo Señora Rios. Tu maestra es la Señorita Taylor. Como te llamas?"*

Luz was very glad to hear words she knew. *"Me llamo Luz,"* she answered.

"What did you two say?" the boy asked.

"I said, 'My name is Mrs. Rios. Your teacher is Miss Taylor. What is your name?' The little girl said, 'My name is Luz.'"

"That's a funny name," the boy said. "I never heard it before."

"It's a pretty name," Mrs. Rios said. "Luz means light." She picked Luz up and held her high in the air. "See, Luz. Luz means light." Luz looked up toward the light. She smiled and then she started to laugh.

When Mrs. Rios put Luz down, the children were sitting in a circle around their teacher. Miss Taylor said, "Children, let's play a little game. I'll call the roll. When I call your name, say 'I am here' in the language you know best."

Mrs. Rios spoke in Spanish and told Luz what Miss Taylor had said. Luz nodded and smiled.

Miss Taylor called Wendy, and Wendy
answered, "I am here."
Tyrone said, "I am here."
Dominique said, *"Je suis ici."*
Paul and Robin each said,
"I am here."
Then Luz heard her name.

"Yo estoy aquí," she said softly.

Robin said, "Yo estoy aquí. I am here. Yo estoy aquí. That sounds nice."

All the children said, "Yo estoy aquí." Luz felt
very special and proud.

Then a lady in white wheeled in a lunch wagon and the children sat down at tables. Mrs. Rios filled two plates and sat next to Luz.

Everyone seemed to like the strange things
that Mrs. Rios called hot dogs. But Luz tasted
hers and made a face.

She thought of rice with beans and of her
favorite chicken dish that her grandmother
made. Mrs. Rios looked a little bit like
Grandma, and Mrs. Rios was eating the hot
dogs. Luz took a second bite and then a third.

After lunch the children put on their coats,
lined up, and went outside, where some mothers
were waiting.

Everyone started talking at once. "Snow."
"Snow." "Snow," they said.

Luz had never seen anything like it. She held out her hands and caught the soft, white, wet snowflakes. She held out her tongue and tasted the snow. Then she bent down and touched the white ground.

Dominique and Robin came running. "Look, Luz," Robin said. Dominique and Robin showed Luz how to shape the snow into a hard round ball.

Luz played in the snow and made snowballs
with Robin and Dominique.

Then Luz heard someone call her name. "Luz, Luz," Maria was calling. "Luz, Luz."

Luz smiled and waved to her sister. "Yo estoy aquí," she called. "I am here, Maria. Maria, Maria, I am here."

ROSE BLUE turned to writing children's books while taking a post-graduate course in children's literature at the Bank Street College of Education. The books she read about black children were unreal for the Headstart students she teaches in the Bedford-Stuyvesant section of Brooklyn, New York. She decided to write her own. Her first book, *A Quiet Place,* remains a success with youngsters. Miss Blue followed with *Black, Black, Beautiful Black, How Many Blocks Is the World?* and *Bed-Stuy Beat.* In *I Am Here* she continues to display her sensitivity to the problems of minority children.

MONETA BARNETT grew up in Brooklyn, New York, where she still lives. After graduating from Cooper Union, she began her career as an artist and illustrator of children's books. By using several techniques, she has successfully added a fresh and exciting style to a number of books. In *The City Spreads Its Wings* she demonstrated her extraordinary talent as a portrayer of the urban scene. *I Am Here* is Miss Barnett's second book for Franklin Watts, Inc.

Date Due

FEB 24 '75	MAY 2 '80	OCT 14 '88	
JUL 27 '73	MAR 19 '75	JUL 3 '80	MAR 12 '87
NOV 7 '73	NOV 12 '75	OCT 28 '80	AR 12 '87
NOV 21 '73	FEB 18 '76	NOV 25 '80	SEP 25 '90
FEB 6 '74	MAR 2 '76	MAY 1 '81	MAR 18 '91
FEB 13 '74	MAY 14 '76	JUL 8 '81	MAY 20 '91
MAR 14 '74	OCT 6	MAR 15 '83	JY 28 '92
OCT 1 '74	NOV 16 '76	SEP 23 '88	OC 07 '93
	DEC 6 '76	NOV 4 '88	
NOV 4 '74	FEB 28 '78	MAR 0 8 2005	
DEC 2 '74	OCT 10 '78	AUG 1 2 2005	